THE
FOO...
ALL OUT
ATTACK

JOHN HICKMAN
Illustrated by **NEIL EVANS**

BLOOMSBURY EDUCATION
LONDON OXFORD NEW YORK NEW DELHI SYDNEY

CONTENTS

The Agent   7

Breathe   19

Seeing Red   24

Losing it   33

Burning Bridges   39

Tough Love   47

The Funeral   55

Kicking On   61

Hallowed Turf   67

The Agent

Harry plays the ball through and I'm onto it,
behind the other team's left-back. I look to
cross, but no one is in a good position. I
go past the centre-back, and I'm still looking.

Everyone is marked tight. So I hit the ball with the inside of my left boot. It curls right into the top corner. The keeper had no chance.

It's a hat-trick. The lads crowd around me, everyone is buzzing. This is the youth cup quarter final and we are 4-0 up, with five minutes left.

The ref blows the whistle for full-time, grabs the ball and hands it to me. "You earned it," he says.

As I walk off the pitch, I look around. There must be a few hundred people here. That might not sound like much, but it's the biggest crowd I've played in front of. And they are all clapping and cheering my name. I still can't believe it sometimes. Me, Jackson Law, playing for United's academy.

After the match, once I'm cleaned up, I leave the stadium with Mum and my girlfriend, Lauren. A few of the other lads congratulate me again, before heading off with their families.

"I can't believe how mint you were," says Lauren.

I still can't believe she's my girlfriend sometimes. I've had a thing for her since we were about six. She has dark hair, bobbed on one side and shaved down on the other. She has these big brown sparkly eyes and a cute little stud in her nose. And when she smiles, my insides turn to goo.

When Lauren and I first got together, I had to deal with her evil ex-boyfriend. He even tried to make me rob the United changing rooms. But Lauren was worth all that drama. Even if he did nearly try and kill me.

The only thing I'm gutted about is Granddad not being there. He's not well at the moment. He can hardly walk, he coughs a lot, and has trouble with his breathing. Mum and I keep telling him to go and see the doctor, but he doesn't listen. He never listens.

A man walks up to me. "Excuse me," he says. "Sorry to bother you. Have you got a minute?" He looks sharp, dressed in a nice designer suit, wearing an expensive designer watch. He looks like a film star. "I'm Paul," he says. "Paul Logan."

"I'm an agent," he tells us. He seems to guess that I have no idea who he is. "I represent Jesse Walters – have you heard of him?"

I smile. I have heard of Jesse Walters. He's my favourite United player. He broke into the first team at eighteen and scored two goals on his debut. He's the top scorer in the Premier League this season so far and he's only twenty.

"Is anyone representing you, Jackson?" the man asks.

I'm not really sure what he means but I don't want to look stupid. I shake my head. "Not really," I tell him, hoping I sound cool.

"Well, after watching you out there tonight – and after everything I've heard – it might be something you want to think about," he says.

I think about Wheeler, how he has always said he wants to represent me, but he was just messing around. What does he know about being an agent?

Paul turns to speak to Mum. "I know some agents get a bad press," he says.

"Call me Carol," she tells him. Her face and neck are all blotchy, the way they always get when she's nervous.

"This isn't about money for me. It's about making the right choices for my players – making sure their careers go the way they want. Now, I know you have a temper, Jackson," he says.

I want to tell him I don't have a temper, but I can't lie.

"I like that," he says. "Passion – it can take you that extra mile. But you need to keep it focussed."

"I am," I tell him.

"So I hear," he says. "There's a good story here too. A kid from a difficult background – no offence, I'm from near the Fordwell estate myself."

"How do you know where I live?" I ask.

"I do my research," he says. "You started at the academy late, and it has been a battle for you. People will really get on board with that. You could be a role model."

My mum smiles when he says this. "That's what I've always told him," she says.

"Take this," he says, and he gives me a glossy business card. "Think about what I've said and give me a ring. Nice meeting you all." He gives us a smile, and then heads off.

I stand there, staring at the card, even though I can't really focus. The words blur into thick lines of grey. The truth is, my head is spinning with thoughts of agents and playing for United and England. Playing with Jesse Walters.

"Did you see his watch?" asks Lauren. "Pretty bling, wasn't it?"

"Probably talking a few thousand pounds," I say.

"For a watch!" says Mum. I worry for a moment she might have a heart attack.

Back at the flats, I'm bouncing around on the landing, holding onto my match-ball, while Mum unlocks the front door. I can't wait to get inside and tell Granddad about the match, about the hat-trick and about meeting the agent. As soon as the door is open, I rush in. "Granddad," I shout. "Wait till you hear this."

He's not in the living room. The TV is on – some old comedy show – but Granddad is not there. I put the match-ball down on the sofa, nice and safe.

"Granddad?" I shout again.

I stick my head in the kitchen. No sign of him in there. I knock on the bathroom door. "Granddad, are you in there?" I ask.

"I'll go and get tea," says Mum, as she goes past.

"Yeah, cool," I say. I try the door, and it opens.

Then I see him.

Granddad.

He's lying on the bathroom floor.

Breathe

I just freeze.

Then I scream for Mum.

She rushes in. "What is it, Jacks..." She sees him too. "Dad? Dad!" She goes down on her knees and lifts his head.

"Is he alright?" I ask.

She leans down, puts her ear against his chest.

"Is he?" I ask again. I can hear the creak in my throat and feel the sting in my eyes.

"He's breathing," she says. "Dad, can you hear me?"

He tries to reply, but he can't get the words out.

"Call an ambulance, Jackson," she says and I just stare at her like my brain is frozen.

"Jackson!" she calls.

I pull my phone out, unlock it. My hands are shaking. I do my best to dial 9 9 9.

A few hours later, Granddad is in hospital, in a gloomy little room. He's hooked up to a machine.

I sit at one side of his bed and Mum sits at the other. She holds his hand and says nothing, and I just stare at the floor. I can hardly look up. The light is so bright in here, it hurts my head. Plus I don't want to see him, not like this. Not with that oxygen mask on his face. It makes this breathing sound, then two heartbeats. It makes me think of Darth Vader.

The truth is, I'm really scared. What will I do if I lose him?

He has been like a dad to me. I wish it was me in that bed, with that thing stuck to my face. I'm young, healthy. But Granddad has been getting weaker and weaker these last few months. I should have made him see the doctor. I should have dragged him there myself.

Someone knocks at the door. "Could I have a word with you?" asks a doctor. He's young, with floppy hair and big glasses. Dr Abbot, the name badge on his shirt says. "Your dad has very weak lungs I'm afraid," he says to Mum. "It's a bad case of pneumonia."

"Will he be OK?" I ask.

The doctor smiles at me, and nods. "We are doing everything we can."

Seeing Red

A few days later, there is an under-sixteens game against County. Granddad is still in hospital and he's the only thing on my mind. I keep thinking about him in that bed with that machine breathing for him. What if he doesn't recover? What if he does recover? How much worse off will he be?

In the changing rooms, before the game, all the lads are getting ready. Ryan sits next to me. He looks the same as he did when I first met him. He has still got that same skinhead.

"Alright, mate," he says. "What did you do with your match-ball the other day?"

"Nothing," I tell him.

"I would have framed it," he says.

"As if you would ever score a hat-trick," calls Ollie from the other side of the changing room. His blond hair is brushed back – he always has the latest style. He gives me this massive smile, with his super-white teeth.

"Everything alright, Jax?" Ollie asks me.

"Yeah, man," I lie.

Then Liam, our coach, comes in. He gives us his pre-match talk, and the next thing I know, I'm out on the pitch.

It's a cold Wednesday evening. I know I probably shouldn't be here but I need something to distract me from worrying about Granddad. And anyway, if I'm going to be a pro and play for England with Jesse Walters, I need to be able to play no matter what is going on at home. I need to be professional.

The ref blows his whistle and the game kicks off. I get the ball and straight away their number 6 is on me. He's an ugly thing, like a bulldog. He has got a scruffy beard and arms covered in tattoos. I shield the ball from him, but he kicks at my ankles, grabs onto my shirt. I try to shake him off, but he holds on.

I look to the ref, but he doesn't seem to think I've been fouled.

I keep the ball, but the number 6 is still kicking, still grabbing. I try to turn. One way, then the other way. I try to get away from him but he's still holding on.

Then I lose it and shove him away from me.

Now the ref blows his whistle. He holds his arms out wide, signalling for a free kick.

"At last," I say.

He points in the direction of my goal. The free kick has gone to County.

"To them?" I shout. "Are you joking?"

The number 6 grabs the ball and shoves me out of the way.

"Move away from the ball now," says the ref.

"Are you actually stupid?" I ask.

"I'm sorry," says the ref. "What was that?"

I say again, "Are you actually stupid?"

"Enough of your lip," he tells me. "Any more, and you're booked."

Ryan jogs over, pulls me away. "Come on, man," he says. "We've only just kicked off."

"Jackson!" Liam shouts from the sidelines. "Focus."

Their number 6 is at me for the whole game. Little kicks, little digs. The ref gives me nothing. I do my best to hold my temper, but it's hard.

Then Ollie knocks the ball to me. I beat a man with a step-over, and I'm running towards their goal. I see him, the number 6, charging at me. I'm going to play it through his legs, and make him look like the mug he is.

But I don't get a chance.

He jumps in, two-footed.

I jump the tackle, but he catches my foot.

I clatter against the grass.

Even though I'm in pain, I quickly get up again. He gets up too, the mug.

"What are you doing?" I ask. "You could have broken my leg."

He just grins at me.

My temper boils over.

I grab hold of his shirt and pull him in.

Then I nut him.

His nose pops.

Blood everywhere.

All over his face. All over his shirt and all over me. Players rush in and everything is a blur.

Losing it

Next thing I know, I'm sitting in the changing rooms, with Liam standing in front of me.

"I just don't understand," he says. "What were you thinking?"

I don't answer.

"Things have been going so well," he goes on. "You played great in the cup game last week, and I know Paul spoke to you about being your agent. I thought you had your temper under control."

"You thought wrong," I say quietly.

"What was that?" he asks.

"You thought wrong," I say again only a little bit louder than last time.

"What has got into you?" he asks. "Is something going on at home?"

"None of your business," I tell him.

"Well, that's where you are wrong," he says. "When something is bothering one of my players, it **is** my business."

"You don't care," I tell him.

"How do you mean?" he asks.

"You don't care about me," I say. "All you care about is winning – getting three points."

"That's not true," he tells me. "You know that's not true."

"Well," I say. "It's all you ever go on about."

"My players come before anything else," he says. "I've taken a big risk with you."

"How?" I ask and I can feel myself getting hot with anger.

"You were fifteen when you joined," he tells me. "Clubs don't take fifteen-year-olds on. Not clubs this big, at any rate."

"So?"

"So," he says. "I took a chance with you. I knew about your anger, and your bad attitude. But we worked through it, because I thought you were worth it. I thought you could make it."

"Maybe you were wrong," I say.

"Maybe I was," he says shaking his head.

"So what are you doing then?" I ask. "Why are you wasting your time on a loser like me?"

He doesn't answer.

"Come on, tell me," I demand.

"Look, maybe I shouldn't have said all those things," he says. "But I thought we were getting somewhere, **really** getting somewhere."

I stare at him, but I don't speak.

"I don't know what is going on with you," he says. "Maybe you just need some time out."

I stare down at the floor. All I can see is Granddad, hooked up to that horrible machine.

"Maybe you could talk with our counsellor," he goes on. "It might help, talking with someone. I can set up a meeting, if you like?"

"So you think I'm some kind of nutcase?" I shout at him.

"I didn't say that," says Liam.

"Forget this," I say. I jump up. And before I know what I'm doing, I tell Liam, "I've had it."

"What do you mean, 'had it'?" he asks.

"I've had it with this club," I tell him. "I've had it with you."

Burning Bridges

The next day, after me and Mum have been
to visit Granddad, I sit in my room watching
United highlights on my laptop. I'm not really
watching though. I just stare at the card Paul
the agent gave me. The intercom buzzes
in the hallway and I can hear Mum answer it.

After a moment, she knocks on my door.

"Am I OK to come in?" she asks.

"Yeah," I tell her.

She opens the door and sticks her head in. "Paul the agent is here. Did you know he was coming?"

Paul sits with us in the living room, holding a mug of tea Mum has made him. "It was really good to hear from you, Jackson," he says. "I'm glad you called."

Mum looks at me, but she doesn't say anything.

"Have you thought about what I said?" he asks.

"Yeah," I tell him.

"So what do you reckon?" he asks. "Are you up for signing with me?"

"No," I tell him.

"OK," he says slowly and he looks over at Mum.

"To be honest, Paul," she says. "I didn't even know he had called you. It's not a good time for us," she goes on. "My dad has been taken into hospital, and we are both worried about him."

"I'm really sorry to hear that," he says. "I can call back another day, when you have had more time to think."

"That might be better," says Mum.

"I've had enough time," I tell him. "I don't need an agent."

"OK," says Paul. "Are you going on your own?"

"No," I tell him. "I've quit. So I don't need an agent."

"You've quit?" he asks.

"Yeah," I tell him.

"He doesn't mean it," says Mum. "He's just upset."

"No," I tell her. "I mean it."

* * *

Later that evening, I'm outside, at the back of the flats. I'm blasting the match-ball against the wall, over and over again. I needed to get outside and get some fresh air.

Then I see Lauren, out of the corner of
my eye.

"Hey, Jax," she says. "Your mum said you
might be down here."

"She knows me so well," I say.

"I've been trying to get in touch," she says.
"So has Wheeler."

I don't say anything.

"I made you these," she says. She opens
a biscuit tin and shows me some cupcakes.
"I thought they might cheer you up."

"Thanks," I say, but I don't mean it. I know
I'm being mean, but I can't help it. I just
want to make everyone else hurt the way
I'm hurting.

"I know you're upset," she says. "But it's not fair what you're doing, shutting everyone out."

"And you think it's fair what has happened to my granddad?" I ask.

"No, of course not," she says. "Did I say that?"

"I know for a fact Mum asked you to come," I say.

"She didn't."

"I'm sick of everyone thinking they know what is best," I tell her. "Telling me what to do. No one has any idea."

"I'm supposed to be your girlfriend," she says.

"Yeah, supposed to be," I tell her.

"What does that mean?"

"Why don't you just go?" I say. "Leave me alone."

"Because I don't want to," she tells me.

"Well, I want you to," I say sharply.

"Do you really mean that?" she asks.

I don't answer. I just watch as she hurries away. Even though she has her back to me, I know she's crying.

I want to call her back to say sorry.

But I don't.

Instead, I punch the wall with my fist.

Tough Love

The next day, me and Mum sit with Granddad in the hospital. For the first time in ages, he's not just sleeping all day and he's able to talk. Sort of. It's difficult for him, with his breathing.

"So…" he says. "How has everyone been?" His voice is all rough and croaky.

"Oh, you know," says Mum. She looks over at me, and I feel really guilty.

"Have you been behaving?" he asks me.

I don't answer.

"He has just been worried about you," says Mum.

"About me?" asks Granddad. "I'm fit as a fiddle." Then he coughs – a loud, nasty cough.

Mum jumps up out of her chair. "Are you OK?" she asks. "Anything I can do?"

"I'm fine," he says. "Can you give us a minute?" he asks. "Me and the boy."

She kisses him on the cheek, smiles at me and leaves the room.

Granddad waits for the door to close, before he says anything. "Your mum told me," he says. "What you did."

"What have I done?" I ask.

"Giving up the football," he says.

I don't answer.

"What have you done that for?" he asks.

I just look down at my feet.

"I can't understand it," he says. "After all that hard work?"

"What's the point?" I ask him.

"How do you mean?"

"I'm never going to get anywhere, am I?" I tell him.

"What makes you think that?"

I don't answer.

"You're a big idiot," he says. "Of course you will. I wouldn't have spoken to Arthur, the United scout, if I didn't think you were good."

My heart stops a moment. I think back to where it all started – playing football with Wheeler in the park. I remember Arthur, this old man, standing there, with his little dog, watching us. I think about him giving me his card, telling me he was a scout. I didn't believe him. Then I think about Granddad taking me to my trial, being there with me all the way. My lucky break with United is all thanks to Granddad.

"So it was you who phoned Arthur?" I ask.

"I did," Granddad says. "Because I believe in you... I know you can make it."

I feel even worse now.

"But even if you don't make the first team," Granddad says. "I'm so proud of you. The lad you are... the man you will be. I couldn't be any prouder if I tried."

I feel like I might cry.

"I know you struggle to talk about things. You get that from me," he says. "But you need to stop bottling things up. It will do you no good."

Now I really feel like crying, but I keep the tears inside me. "How can I make it, if you're not there?" I ask.

"Come here, you big lump," he says. "Give us a hug."

I go over, hug him.

"You've done it all on your own," he says. "All I did was give you a shove. I want you to promise me... promise me, that whatever happens, you will never give up on your dream... OK?"

I nod my head.

"Say it," he tells me. "Promise me."

"I promise."

* * *

The next day, I'm in my bedroom, playing football on my games console, when I hear something. It sounds like someone crying.
I pause the game and walk out of my room. As I walk along the hallway, the sound gets louder.

In the living room, Mum is crying. Her phone is on the floor.

"What is it, Mum?" I whisper.

She stares up at me and shakes her head. "It's your granddad," she says. "He couldn't fight the pneumonia any more."

My legs go weak. I sit down on the arm of Granddad's chair and I just feel numb. I want to speak, say something, but I don't. I can't. It's like my breath and my voice have been stolen from me.

The Funeral

A week or so later, I'm in the church, sitting at the front with Mum and Lauren. I know Lauren is still really mad at me, but she agreed to come when Mum asked her.

I am so glad she's here. It makes me feel
better having her around. I just hope she will
forgive me for being so mean.

I've never been to a funeral before. It
is horrible. Everyone is so quiet and sad,
whispering to each other. All Granddad's mates
from the pub and the taxi firm are here,
people I haven't seen in years. When the
vicar talks, all I want to do is laugh or scream,
but I don't.

Afterwards, we stand outside the church,
and people come up and tell us they're sorry,
and what a great bloke my granddad was.

Liam comes over, dressed in a dark suit.
He looks strange not wearing his tracksuit,
and I almost don't recognise him.

"I'm really sorry," he says to my mum. "Sorry to hear about your granddad," he tells me.

I nod. "Cheers."

"The lads all send their best," he says. "The place hasn't been the same without you."

I think about United, the lads. I feel gutted for what I've done, what I've given up.

"Take care, both of you," he says. He walks away.

The words Granddad said to me the last time I spoke with him fill my head.

"Wait," I say. "Wait a minute."

He stops, turns back.

"Sorry for quitting," I tell him. "I didn't mean it. I want to come back."

"Can I?" I ask him. "Can I come back?"

He looks at Mum and smiles. "Of course you can. Whenever you're ready."

"I'm ready now," I tell him.

"There's no rush," he says.

"I'm ready," I repeat. "I'm not quitting again," I tell him. "I'm never quitting again."

"Don't," he says. "No matter what." He winks at me, nods at Mum and Lauren and walks off.

Mum gives me a hug, and kiss on the head. "You've been so brave," she says.

"I haven't," I tell her. "I have been a total idiot. Sorry Lauren. Sorry for what I said. I was out of order."

Even at a funeral she looks great, in her black dress with these little lacy bits. She gives me this smile, like she's really sad. And I can't help thinking that this is it, we are over and she's only here at the funeral because she's a good person.

I feel a pain worse than when her ex thumped me in the guts. I've blown it, I know I have. I'm such an idiot.

Kicking On

A few days later, I rock up at the academy ground and walk over to the pitch where the lads are training. I watch them, as they play a game we call tennis, knocking the ball to each other, keeping it in the air with their feet and heads.

Ryan and Ollie jog over when they see me. "How are you doing?" asks Ollie.

"I'm alright," I tell him. "Better than I was."

"Sorry about your Granddad," says Ryan. "He was a sound geezer."

"Yeah," I say, remembering the first time I trained with the team and how Ryan called my granddad a freak.

"When are you coming back?" asks Ryan.

"Now," I tell him.

They look at one another, like that is a bad idea.

"Have you spoken with Liam?" asks Ollie.

"Not yet," I tell him. Then I call out, "Liam, you got a minute?"

***

Liam and I watch the lads from the sidelines as Darren, Liam's assistant, supervises a game of five-a-side.

"It might be a bit early," he says. "With everything that has happened."

"I just need to get back out there and get on with things," I tell him.

He stares at me, but doesn't say anything.

"It's what my granddad would have wanted," I tell him.

"Probably," he says. "It's just, I've seen what happens when you get on the pitch and your head isn't in the game. It doesn't usually end well, does it?"

"No."

"It's not like you can play a match for a while at any rate," he says. "You are serving a five-game ban."

"Five games?!"

"You should count yourself lucky," he says. "The FA wanted a ten-game ban."

"Really?" I ask.

"Really," he tells me. "You head-butted a player."

"I'm sorry," I say.

"It's done now," he says. "Just don't ever do it again. I spoke with Paul too – a real shame what happened."

"Yeah," I say and I feel gutted about the whole thing.

"There will be other agents though," he tells me, and I feel a bit better.

"I was thinking," I tell him. "About what you said, about that counsellor."

"Oh yeah?" he says.

"Do you think it could help?" I ask.

"Well, I'm not an expert," says Liam, "but it can't be a bad idea to talk to someone who understands all this. It definitely helps me when I talk – can't shut me up in fact. Why don't you have a session or two, see how it goes?"

"OK," I tell him. "Sign me up or whatever."

He smiles. "I'll sign you up. And in future, if there is anything, anything at all the matter, you come to talk to me."

I nod and smile.

"I mean it," he says. "If you need anything, my door is always open."

"Actually, Liam," I say. "There is one thing."

Hallowed Turf

A few days later, Lauren, Mum and I walk down the tunnel and out onto United's pitch. Even though the stadium is empty, it still feels amazing to be here. On the pitch where so many of my favourite players have played.

It gives me a proper buzz and goosebumps all down my neck and arms.

The three of us walk towards the goals at the Clock End. This is the end where all the hardcore fans sit, the end opposition teams hate to face. It's where Granddad used to sit, back when he had a season ticket. Before he got too sick to come to games.

"Do you want to do it?" asks Mum.

I stare at the goal line, think about all the games Granddad and I watched together. All the goals that crossed this line. "Yeah," I say.

Mum hands me an urn. We got it especially for him, in United's colours.

"What should I do?" I ask.

"Just pour it out, I guess," she tells me.

I unscrew the lid of the urn and tip Granddad's ashes gently along the goal line. I watch as the grey powder hits the grass and paint, and think how much Granddad would have loved this – bringing good luck to United strikers and stopping all the opposition's goals.

Once I'm done, I screw the lid up.

"He would have loved this, wouldn't he?" says Lauren.

"He would," I tell her.

She takes my hand and squeezes it tight, like she might have forgiven me for being horrible to her.

"Imagine how he will feel when you run out for real," says Mum. "When you're playing for the first team."

I turn slowly around looking at the huge stadium. It's amazing. I can't wait until I walk out with the first team, just like Mum says.

"Granddad would be proud of you no matter what," says Mum.

I smile and nod and I think I might cry, but I quickly stop myself. Then I think about what Granddad said, about how I bottle everything up all the time.

A tear runs down my cheek and I cry. Just a little bit.

"Come here," says Mum and she hugs me.

Bonus Bits!

Guess Who?

Each piece of information below is about one of the characters in the story. Can you match them up? You can check your answers at the end of this section.

1 Jackson Law

2 Lauren

3 Granddad

4 Paul Logan

5 Jesse Walters

6 Carol (Mum)

7 Ryan

8 Ollie

9 Liam

A Has a skinhead haircut

B represents Jesse Walters

C his Granddad is poorly

D always has the latest hairstyle

E has a nose stud

F scored two goals in his debut

G tells Jackson he took a chance on him

H spoke to Arthur the United scout

I has a blotchy face and neck when nervous

"BOTTLING THINGS UP"

This is a common saying: when a person "bottles things up" it means that they refuse to talk about things that make them worried, upset or angry.

They keep the worries inside them. This can often make the worries seem worse than they are, because the person doesn't talk to someone else about them and doesn't get perspective (another point of view) on the problem.

Another popular saying is "a problem shared is a problem halved". This means that if you talk about a problem with someone else it can seem much less troubling or scary. Often you can find a solution or way forward.

Jackson, in this story, needs to learn to talk about his problems, and asks for counselling to talk about his problems rather than just getting angry inside.

ISSUES

This book deals with a very difficult issue that all of us, at some point, have to face – the death of someone close to us.

This is certainly a time when it is important to talk about your feelings with someone. This can often be done with family and friends but you might want to talk to someone independent to get a sense of what is happening to you emotionally.

Here are some useful websites/contacts:

Childline

Childline is a free, 24-hour counselling service for everyone under 18. Childline says, "You can talk to us about anything. No problem is too big or too small. We're on the phone and online. However you choose to contact us, you're in control. It's free, confidential and you don't have to give your name if you don't want to."

www.childline.org.uk / 0800 1111

Child Bereavement UK

"If someone important to you has just died, or you have just found they are very seriously ill, you are not alone and you can get help and support."

https://childbereavementuk.org/young-people/

0800 02 888 40

WHAT NEXT?

Have a think about these questions after reading this story:

- How do you deal with worries that you have? Do you bottle them up or share them with your friends or family?
- Why is it important not to quit when you are finding things hard?

ANSWERS to GUESS WHO?

1C, 2E, 3H, 4B, 5F, 6I, 7A, 8D, 9G

Look out for more of Jackson's adventures!

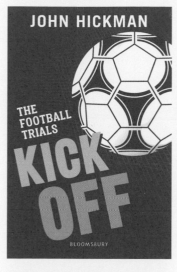

978-1-4729-4411-5

978-1-4729-4415-3

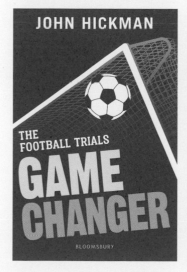

978-1-4729-4419-1

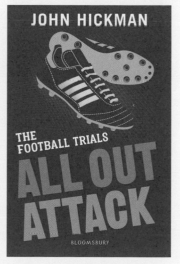

978-1-4729-4423-8